Mia

Mia is Lost

A Mia the Kitten Adventure, 1

JK KEANE

Illustrations by Sue Richards

YOUCAXTON
PUBLICATIONS

For Kayleigh and Jessica and all children
who love animals and forests,
-you are the future.

Alone we can do so little;
together we can do so much.
- *Helen Keller* -

Contents

Chapter 1

Mia Moves House

Mia scratched at the bars of her carrier as hard as she could, but it was hopeless. The door just wouldn't budge, not even a little. She licked her sore paws and sighed. She'd been stuck in the dark carrier on the car's backseat for hours. Her owners, a young couple called Caroline and Steve, had tricked her into it that morning by hiding treats, right at the back and she'd been in there ever since.

Finally, the car came to a stop. Caroline got out and grabbed the carrier. 'Where shall I put the kitten?' she asked.

Mia felt a bit sick after the journey and couldn't wait to get out and enjoy some fresh air and open space.

'Put her in one of the bedrooms,' Steve said. 'She'll just get in the way otherwise.'

Mia couldn't believe what she was hearing. That wasn't fair. They had kept her in the stupid carrier all day and now she was going to be shut in a bedroom. She wanted to run around and explore.

The carrier wobbled as Caroline took it upstairs, making Mia feel dizzy. As soon as the door opened, she shot out and jumped onto the nearest windowsill. Caroline came over to stroke her. Usually, Mia loved nothing more than a bit of attention, but as she was still upset, she glared at Caroline and even hissed, showing off her sharp teeth.

'Oh Mia, don't be like that,' Caroline moaned. 'I promise you'll soon get used to the new house. There's a huge garden that leads straight into a forest.'

Mia's whiskers twitched. She had pretended not to be listening to Caroline, but she was curious now. What was a forest? Maybe it was obvious? She looked out of the window. Directly outside the house, she spotted a terrace and a lawn. They looked the same as at her old place, only a lot bigger. When she saw the rest of the garden her eyes widened in surprise. It seemed wild, with long grass and lots of flowers. A single tree with pretty pink blossoms stood proudly in the middle.

Mia spotted a yellow butterfly and followed its flight, itching to chase it. After a few moments spent watching the butterfly, her gaze drifted towards the back of the garden, where she saw a fence with a rusty gate in the corner. Behind the fence were trees, lots of trees. Was that the forest? She wasn't sure, but her tail began to swish from side to side, like a whip that had suddenly come alive.

Mia watched a butterfly

Later that evening, Steve walked into the bedroom. Mia was dozing on the windowsill, but she woke in an instant and jumped to the floor when she heard him arrive.

'Hello, my midnight princess,' he said.

Mia liked that nickname. It suited her because her fur was all black. She rubbed herself against Steve's legs. When he stroked her in her favourite spot, just behind her ears, Mia closed her eyes and purred happily.

Steve smiled and opened the bedroom door wide. 'Go on, you little rascal, time to explore.'

Mia's eyes lit up. She dashed through his legs but quickly lost her footing and skidded into a box that had been abandoned on the landing.

'Ouch!' she shouted. She was still excited, but she moved a bit more carefully after that. She spent the evening roaming around the new house before falling asleep on Caroline's lap, exhausted but happy. Her owners spent the next few days cleaning and decorating their new home. Mia tried to help as best as she could. During the second day in the new house, she jumped on a curtain rail and ripped the new curtains. Of course, she hadn't meant to. It was an accident.

Another time, she got into trouble for adding white footprints to the polished wooden floorboards. That wasn't exactly her fault either. She had dunked her paws in a tray of white stuff that she thought was milk, although, sadly, it turned out to be paint. Steve had shouted and poured lots of water over her when he noticed. Mia still trembled when she thought about the forced bath in the kitchen sink. She decided to stay well away from paint after that.

In addition to getting in the way a lot, Mia spent hours sitting on the windowsill and gazing out at the garden. So far, she had seen three cats out there. The first one, a huge ginger tomcat, seemed to spend most of his time on the roof of the shed. The second cat appeared to live in the house next door. Mia had never seen such a colourful cat before and thought the combination of white, black and brown fur looked beautiful. Still, it was the third cat that intrigued her the most. He was a male kitten with black and grey stripes. He seemed only slightly bigger than Mia. She had seen him climbing the tree in the garden as well as racing about chasing blackbirds.

Mia hoped that the other cats would like her. She remained curious about the forest behind the garden fence and wanted to explore there. Playing outside would be much more fun than being stuck inside.

Mia liked to rub herself against Steve's legs

One game that Mia particularly enjoyed involved sneaking up on her owners and making them jump. Caroline was the most fun when playing this game because she shrieked louder than Steve. A few weeks after the move, Mia hid halfway up the staircase. Her tail swished from side to side as she shuffled into position. When Caroline walked by, carrying a glass of orange juice, Mia pounced. She managed to land on Caroline's shoulder but had to dig her claws in to keep her balance.

'Aaarrrrgghh!' Caroline shrieked.

She dropped her glass, which shattered on the wooden floor, splashing orange juice all over the newly painted walls.

'Mia, when I get my hands on you...' Caroline shouted.

Mia wasted no time and fled to her safest hiding place under the sofa. She felt a bit guilty. She hadn't meant to cause trouble. She was just so bored. She wanted to play and explore, not stay in the house all the time.

Steve came running from the kitchen. 'What happened?' he asked.

Caroline burst into tears. 'Mia's out of control, that's what happened.'

'Maybe it's time we let her out,' Steve said.

Caroline wiped away her tears. 'Do you think she's big enough? There are other cats out there and she's still so small.'

'She's twenty weeks old now. Other people let their kittens outside much earlier.'

Mia's ears pricked up. Were they going to finally let her out?

'She's certainly feisty enough to look after herself, the little devil,' Caroline said.

Steve grinned. 'I feel sorry for the other cats already.'

Chapter 2

Mia's Garden

The next morning, after she'd gobbled down her breakfast, Mia rushed straight to the cat flap. She knew how it worked as the old house had one that led into a small conservatory. She pushed her paws against it, but it didn't open. She turned around and glared at Steve. They had promised to let her out! Had they forgotten?

'I swear that kitten understands every word we say,' he laughed as he walked to the cat flap.

Caroline stroked Mia's back. 'Be careful out there. Stay in the garden and come straight back if any of the big cats chase you.'

'Stop fussing,' Steve said. 'Let her go.'

He unlocked the hatch of the cat flap and winked at Mia.

'Have fun, my little black panther.'

Mia was itching to go. She jumped through the catflap, buzzing with excitement. As she landed on the terrace, she stopped, suddenly unsure. Where should she start? She tried to take it all in—the smell of the flowers, the gentle breeze and the sun on her coat. It all felt great. Should she chase some butterflies or climb the tree or maybe ambush the blackbird that was bobbing about in front of her? So many choices. Then she spotted the big ginger cat lying on top of the shed. Maybe he would show her around?

Mia climbed up the fence near the shed. The ginger cat turned his big head and stared at her. He really was huge, about twice her size. She swallowed and kept her eyes fixed on him, ready to race back to the house if necessary.

'Hi, I'm Mia,' she said quietly. The ginger cat just stared at her. She couldn't read his body language. Was he friendly?

'I've just moved here. What's your name?' she tried again, a little louder this time.

'Rosco,' the ginger cat said after a pause. He had a deep voice that sounded rather grumpy.

'Can you play with me? Or show me around?' Mia asked.

Rosco shook his head. 'No, leave me alone. Find someone else to play with.'

Well, that didn't go very well, Mia thought. What a shame. Rosco was a powerful cat who would be a useful friend if she got into trouble, and she was an expert at getting into trouble. But then she shrugged. Who wanted to be friends with a grumpy old cat like that? She could look after herself. She jumped off the fence and headed for the long grass at the back of the garden.

Rosco dozed on the shed

Soon afterwards, Mia spotted the colourful cat she had seen before. The cat was sunbathing on the terrace of the house next door. Mia took a deep breath and approached her carefully. Maybe this cat would be nicer than Rosco?

'Hello, I'm Mia. I've just moved here and this is my first day outside.'

'My name is Melissa,' the colourful cat answered slowly. She cleaned her front paws, yawned and then lay down in a sunny spot with her eyes half closed.

'Can we be friends?' Mia asked. She thought Melissa looked beautiful.

The older cat opened one eye and looked at Mia. 'No, I don't think so. I don't run around or play games. I don't like getting dirty or sweaty.'

Mia was disappointed. She had failed to make new friends. Who was going to join her on her big adventures in the forest? The garden didn't seem so beautiful and fun anymore. Mia dragged her paws towards the cherry tree. She jumped up onto one of the lower branches and sighed. No one wanted to play with her. Her head dropped and she closed her eyes.

'Watch out!'

Mia nearly fell off her branch. She hadn't been paying attention and so had failed to spot that a tabby kitten was sitting in the tree above her. He was balanced on a thin branch, high up in the tree.

The tabby bowed his head. 'Sorry to startle you. I couldn't resist...'

He jumped down from his branch and sat beside her. He looked friendly, although he didn't seem able to sit still for very long.

'I'm new here. My name is Mia,' she said as she shuffled a bit to the side to make room for him on the branch.

'I'm called Joker,' he said. 'Why do you look so sad?'

'Nobody wants to play with me,' Mia sighed. A single tear dropped to the ground as she told him about her encounters with Rosco, the big ginger cat, and Melissa, the colourful cat.

'I'm not surprised,' Joker said. 'I think they both prefer snoozing to playing.'

Joker tried to balance on two paws but failed and almost fell out of the tree. Mia giggled and her eyes began to sparkle. Maybe she had finally found a friend?

Joker tilted his head and looked at her. 'How old are you anyway?'

'Five months,' she said, sitting up as tall as she could.

'Wow, we're the same age. That's cool.'

Mia smiled. She liked Joker. He seemed a bit clumsy, but she didn't mind. He was good fun.

Melissa licked her paw

'Would you like to be my friend?' she asked. 'We could play together every day.'

Joker grinned. 'I'd love to be your friend!'

'Great, we'll go on amazing adventures.' Mia's whiskers twitched as she thought about how much fun they would have in the forest.

Joker was a bit worried when he heard Mia talk about adventures. He wasn't brave and tried to stay out of trouble as much as possible, although he wanted to be friends with Mia. Her black shiny coat looked beautiful, and he loved the way she gazed at him with her gorgeous green eyes. He didn't want to disappoint her and so made up his mind to be braver in the future. For now, he would concentrate on amusing her. He pretended to fall out of the tree. Luckily, he managed to land on his feet at the last moment.

Mia laughed and the two kittens began to explore. She followed Joker through a secret passage under the shed that led into next door's garden. It was just wide enough for them to squeeze through. They played by the pond next door, getting their paws wet and muddy. At one point, they even climbed onto the roof of Mia's house.

In the afternoon, they played hide and seek and then chased each other through the grass until they were both out of breath. Joker was a bit stronger and could jump higher, but Mia was faster and could climb better.

'That was fun!' she said, once she could breathe again.

'Fantastic!' Joker replied. He rolled onto his belly and lay still for the first time in hours.

Mia gazed longingly at the trees behind the garden fence. 'Tomorrow we'll have to go into the forest. You must know a lot of spooky places in there?'

'Sure,' Joker said. 'I've been in the forest loads of times.'

'I'm glad you're brave,' Mia said. 'Some of my brothers and sisters were proper chickens. They would never go exploring, not even inside the house.'

Joker swallowed and suddenly looked worried. Mia didn't notice. Her eyes were glued on the forest. Tomorrow, the real adventure would begin. But first, she needed food. Mia yawned. It had been a busy day. She was looking forward to her dinner, her bed and maybe a cuddle with Caroline or Steve.

Chapter 3

The Forest

Mia woke early the next morning. She had slept on a pillow between Caroline and Steve. Cosy and warm, it was her favourite place to spend the night. The first rays of sunlight sneaked in through the window. She yawned and snuggled on top of Steve's head. She liked to wake up slowly and doze for a while before getting up, but then she remembered: Joker was going to show her the forest. Suddenly wide awake, she jumped up and started prodding Steve with her paw.

'No, Mia. Leave me alone. It's too early.' With a groan, Steve rolled over onto his other side.

Mia sighed. She was hungry and could hear her tummy rumbling. She shook her head in frustration, but Steve had gone back to sleep. She frowned when he began to snore, as it would be almost impossible to wake him now.

Mia didn't give up. She tried rubbing her nose against Caroline's face and purring loudly.

'Mia, go back to sleep,' Caroline mumbled.

Mia spotted Steve's feet sticking out of the duvet at the bottom of the bed. Her eyes lit up. That would work. She jumped to the end of the bed and began to lick his toes. However, despite her best efforts, Steve just snored louder. Mia sat down and chewed her lower lip. How could she wake him up? Joker was probably already outside, waiting for her.

Mia tried to wake up Steve

In the end, she pounced on Steve's right foot and bit his big toe. It wasn't a hard bite, more of a quick nip really, but it proved very effective.

'Aargh!' Steve screamed as he jumped out of the bed.

'Mia, you're a bad cat, a very bad cat,' he grumbled, hopping on one foot. Mia felt a bit guilty and hoped that he wouldn't stay angry for long. She rubbed herself against his legs, tail pointing straight up in the air.

'You're impossible, you little rascal,' Steve said as he followed her down the stairs and into the kitchen. Great! Time for breakfast. Mia meowed loudly and weaved in and out between his legs. Steve was smiling now.

'Let me get to the cat food, you silly kitten.'

He opened a pouch and squeezed the food into her dish. Mia quickly gobbled it all up and then rushed through the cat flap. Outside, the morning air was cool. Thousands of tiny water droplets covered the lawn, glittering in the early sunshine. Mia looked around the garden and was disappointed that she couldn't see any sign of Joker. Where was the tabby kitten?

She tiptoed through the wet grass to ask Rosco, who lay in his usual place on the shed roof.

'Rosco, have you seen Joker?'

'Mmmm...' the big cat grunted. After a pause, he sighed and answered in a grumpy voice. 'No, I haven't. It was lovely and quiet until you disturbed my morning snooze.'

Mia's whiskers twitched as they always did when she was excited. Her eyes darted towards the trees behind the garden fence. 'We're exploring the forest today,' she said. 'Joker's going to show me around.'

Rosco's head shot up and Mia retreated a few steps in surprise. The big ginger cat glared at her.

'Listen to me!' Rosco thundered. 'The forest is no place for kittens. There are animals in there that enjoy eating little cats like you for breakfast.'

Mia didn't believe him. 'You're just trying to spoil our fun,' she said. 'I'm not scared. I can run fast and climb well.'

'Suit yourself, but be warned. The forest is dangerous.'

Mia wasn't listening anymore. She trotted to the tree and jumped onto the lowest branch. Where was Joker? She saw Melissa taking a morning stroll through the garden.

'Melissa, have you seen Joker? He said he'd show me the forest today, but I can't find him.'

Melissa stopped and stared at Mia. 'That is the dumbest thing I've heard in a long time. The two of you will get yourselves killed if you go into that forest.' The older cat had raised her usually soft voice as she spoke.

Melissa warned Mia not to go into the forest

'You're just like Rosco...' Mia moaned as she jumped off the tree.

Mia had never been very patient and the trees behind the garden fence looked inviting. She could hear the leaves rustling and the birds singing. Joker had explored the forest alone. Maybe she should go by herself and then tell him all about it afterwards? He would be really proud of her. Mia had dreamed about adventures for so long. Now was her time to finally go on one!

She moved slowly through the high grass towards the back fence, crouching low and listening for any unusual sounds. Her tail swished from side to side because she was nervous but she kept moving forwards. When she reached the rusty gate, Mia squeezed through a gap between two metal bars. It was darker on the other side, although she could see a faint path leading further into the trees. A black crow sat on an oak tree, staring down at her. The big bird scared Mia.

Seconds later, she heard a rustling sound from somewhere up ahead. She moved forward and followed the path around a bend.

It opened up into a small clearing, where she spotted the source of the rustling noise. A squirrel was digging frantically through a pile of leaves on the forest floor. It stopped suddenly and moved to another spot.

'I hid them here last autumn. Where are they?' the squirrel mumbled. He was so engrossed in the search that he hadn't heard Mia approach.

What was he doing? Mia wasn't sure, but she had an idea what she could do. This would be fun. She crouched low and then jumped high in the air above the squirrel.

'Got you!'

The squirrel fell over backwards. After he rolled back onto his feet, he scurried up the nearest tree while Mia fell about laughing.

'Sorry, Mr Squirrel. I didn't mean to scare you,' she said.

'My name is Freddie, not Mr Squirrel. You almost gave me a heart attack, sneaking up on me like that...' The squirrel now sat a few metres above her on a thin branch. His tail was all bushed up.

'I'm sorry, Freddie. I've never been in a forest before and it's just so exciting. What were you looking for?' Mia asked.

'Hazelnuts, acorns, anything to eat really.' The squirrel rubbed his little belly. 'I haven't had my breakfast yet.'

'I could help you search,' Mia said as she started digging through the leaves. 'Look, I've found one.'

Freddie laughed and joined Mia on the forest floor. 'Thank you. I've never seen a cat dig up acorns. I'm impressed.'

He picked up the acorn that Mia had found with his front paws and started nibbling at it. 'I always forget where I put them. Who are you anyway? I haven't seen you in the forest before.'

Freddie took another tiny bite of the acorn, clearly enjoying his food. Mia thought he looked cute. 'I'm Mia,' she said. 'I live in the house with the big garden and the pretty tree.'

Freddie nodded. 'I know that place. It's great for yummy cherries and tasty hazelnuts.'

'Do you want to be my friend?' Mia asked.

'Only if you promise not to scare me again.'

'I promise,' Mia said, and she meant it. She couldn't believe her luck. She had found a new friend already. A squirrel! Freddie finished eating and then scanned the trees around them. 'I'll show you the forest, but we have to be careful.' His tail twitched as he continued in a whisper. 'Some of the forest animals like to eat squirrels, and who knows, they might fancy some cat meat for a change today.'

Mia felt the hairs rising on her back. 'I'll be careful,' she promised. Her mouth felt dry all of a sudden and her ears flattened a bit, although her eyes still shone with excitement.

Soon after, the two new friends scampered off to explore the forest together. Freddie showed Mia a hollow tree that was lying on the ground. Mia crawled through it and ended up quite dirty.

It was a bit spooky in the forest. They played hide and seek, and afterwards they chased each other through the trees for a while. Freddie was a much better climber than Mia. She couldn't follow him on the thinner branches, but she was faster on the ground and could jump better.

Mia and Freddie played in the trees

They played for hours and ended up deep in the forest, all thoughts of danger forgotten. Late in the afternoon, the pair rested on a nice patch of soft moss at the bottom of some fir trees.

Mia lay on her side with her eyes closed and thought about how the day had been perfect so far. She loved the forest, and she had even managed to find a new friend in Freddie the squirrel. She couldn't wait to tell Joker all about it. He would be so jealous. Maybe tomorrow they could all play together?

Suddenly, she heard Freddie scream at the top of his voice.

'Run, Mia. Run!'

She jumped up and saw Freddie running up a fir tree. He was still shouting.

'Save yourself, Mia!'

Mia was terrified. She was still trying to work out what was happening when she heard loud barking and realised that something big was thundering towards her. She looked around and saw two huge dogs breaking through the undergrowth. Their mouths were wide open and Mia could see their razor-sharp teeth. Even worse, the dogs had spotted Mia and were now charging towards her. Mia's eyes bulged and her heart felt like it was going to explode in her chest. She spun around and ran for her life. Where could she hide?

First, Mia zigzagged around the fir trees. They were of no use to her because they had no branches lower down. Freddie could climb them, but she could not. She spotted a thicket of brambles just a few metres away. Could she make it there in time? She could hear the dogs somewhere behind her. Somewhere close.

Mia ran faster than she had ever run before and then leapt towards the brambles with a mighty jump. She landed in the middle and got stuck on some thorny branches. Fortunately, being small can sometimes be useful. Mia was able to wiggle free and drop down to the forest floor. The dogs were too big to follow and howled in disappointment.

Mia was gasping for air. Her whole body was shaking. She wanted to stop moving but knew she was still in danger. The dogs hadn't given up and were trying to find a way around the brambles. Mia raced through the forest, desperately looking for an escape route. She reached a large meadow covered with bracken. It looked like a good place to hide, although she feared that her scent would give her away.

Without looking behind her, Mia sprinted through the bracken. Her ears flicked backwards to listen for the dogs. Their barks grew louder. They were getting closer. Mia spotted some oak trees at the far end of the meadow. Her panicked eyes lit up and she felt a tiny glimmer of hope. The trees had some lower branches. Her legs were hurting, but she managed a last burst of speed. When she reached the closest oak, Mia raced upwards. Once at the top, she dug her claws into the bark of the tree and tried to catch her breath. Her heart hammered in her chest and she trembled with fear. Wide-eyed, she finally dared to look down.

The dogs had found her and were now jumping up at the tree trunk. They howled and barked so loudly that it made her ears hurt. She saw their long pink tongues and their pointed teeth. Mia shivered. She swallowed and closed her eyes. She knew that the dogs could not get her as long as she stayed up in the tree. She took a few deep breaths. Then she licked herself clean as best as she could. Some of her scratches were bleeding and she felt sore all over.

Mia hated the forest and wished she was back in her safe garden. Where was Freddie? She kept glancing down at the dogs as they prowled around the bottom of the tree, waiting for her to come down. There seemed to be no escape.

How would she ever get back home?

Chapter 4

Joker

Meanwhile, back in Mia's garden, Joker strolled through the long grass. His owners had locked him inside all day, and it had taken him ages to find an open window from which he could escape. Now he was looking for Mia, but he couldn't find her anywhere. How strange. Yesterday she had seemed really keen to visit the forest. Where could she be?

Joker frowned and sighed heavily. Why had he lied to Mia? He had been to the edge of the forest a few times, but he had never dared to explore further. He glanced at the large trees that towered over the garden and shivered.

Joker pondered how to tell Mia that he wasn't very brave and that he thought the forest was too dangerous for small kittens. He barely noticed as a yellow butterfly fluttered close to his head. He walked over to Melissa, who was lying in her usual spot on the terrace.

'Have you seen Mia?' he asked, worry creeping into his heart. 'I can't find her anywhere.'

Melissa cleaned her shiny coat with generous licks of her pink tongue. She glanced at Joker. 'Mia, that little friend of yours? Stupid kitten, so stupid...'

'I know you don't like her, Melissa, but you don't need to be mean,' Joker said, feeling annoyed with the older cat.

'Well, she wandered off into the forest all by herself. What would you call that? I call it extremely stupid.'

Joker's heart skipped a beat. 'Oh, no! Mia's gone into the forest? Why didn't you stop her?'

He felt sick. Mia was in the forest all alone, and he knew he was to blame.

Melissa glared at him. 'I did try to stop her and so did Rosco, but she wouldn't listen to us.' She lowered her head until she was eye to eye with Joker. 'Someone told her that going into the forest would be fun.'

Joker swallowed and looked away. He couldn't meet Melissa's eyes. His stomach hurt and his face felt hot. To make matters worse, Rosco stomped over, his fierce eyes full of anger and his voice cold as ice.

'You lied to Mia and pretended to be a brave explorer,' he growled. 'You, a little kitten who jumps when he sees his own shadow. Unbelievable! Did you mention even once how dangerous the forest can be?'

The big cat stepped closer and Joker shrank back, wishing the ground would swallow him up.

'I wanted her to be my friend,' he whispered. 'She likes adventures, so I pretended to be brave. I just wanted to impress her.'

Melissa tilted her head. 'You should never tell lies. A true friend likes you for who you are, not what you pretend to be. No one is perfect.'

Joker's ears and whiskers drooped. He felt miserable. 'I was going to tell her today and warn her about the danger...' He lifted his head and looked at the older cats. 'When did she go into the forest?'

'Midmorning...' Rosco said.

'But that was hours ago! Why hasn't she come back?'

Rosco shrugged his shoulders. 'We don't know. Maybe something has happened. I went into the forest a few hours ago but didn't find any signs of her.' He sighed and sat down.

Joker stared at the trees that stood dark and gloomy in the fading light. He swallowed the lump that was suddenly in his throat. 'I have to go and look for her. Mia would never have gone into the forest if I hadn't told her that I went there all the time. This is all my fault. I need to make it right.'

He got up and inched towards the garden gate. He took three deep breaths, ignoring the hard knot in his stomach and the hairs standing up all over his back. He needed to be brave and look for Mia. She might be lost.

Suddenly, Melissa stood in front of him. She must have jumped over him from behind. Joker had never seen her move so fast. He was stunned.

'Stop right there!' she said. 'You're not going anywhere. Listen to me, young man. Getting yourself killed is not going to help Mia.'

Rosco appeared beside Melissa, both cats now blocking the way to the gate.

'Melissa is right. You can't go into the forest,' he said.

'But we have to do something,' Joker shouted. 'Please! She needs our help.'

They were interrupted by a squirrel who appeared on top of the fence. It was breathing heavily as if it had run fast and for a long time. The squirrel jumped down onto the grass next to the three cats.

Rosco and Melissa blocked Joker's route into the forest

'Well, look at this. A squirrel with a death wish,' Rosco whispered. His long whiskers twitched and he crouched low, ready to pounce.

The squirrel lifted both front paws high into the air. 'Please don't hurt me. I came to find you. My name is Freddie. I met Mia this morning...'

Joker's ears pricked up. 'Freddie, what happened? Where is Mia?'

Freddie's eyes glistened and his ears and long tail flopped down. 'That's the problem. I don't know where she is. I've lost her.'

He told the three cats about the dogs that had chased Mia. 'She jumped into some brambles and I never saw her again. I looked everywhere and asked all my forest friends, but no one has seen her. I'm worried that she's lost or that the dogs have got her.'

The squirrel looked heartbroken. 'This is all my fault,' he said. 'If I had paid more attention, she would have had time to reach a tree and save herself.' Tears rolled down his cheeks and he quickly wiped them away.

'No, it's all my fault for lying,' Joker sobbed.

'Oh, stop crying, both of you.' Rosco said. 'None of this is helping Mia. What we need is a plan.' The ginger cat tilted his head and looked at Melissa.

'Give me some time. I'm working on it,' she said. Joker gazed at the older cats in surprise. He had always thought that Rosco did the thinking and Melissa did the looking pretty. Had he been wrong?

Melissa turned to the squirrel. 'Freddie, can you show us where you last saw Mia?'

Freddie's head bobbed up and down. 'Yes, of course, but she isn't there. I know the forest well and I searched for Mia for hours before I came here.'

Melissa pursed her lips. 'Mia won't survive in the forest overnight on her own. Our best chance is to work together.'

Rosco shook his head. 'You can't be serious, Melissa. The forest is huge. It would be like asking Freddie to find one special acorn in this garden. He could dig for days and days without finding it.'

Freddie opened his mouth to object, but Melissa was quicker.

'I know that we can't find Mia alone. We need help,' she said.

Joker frowned. Who could help them? Freddie looked equally confused. All of a sudden, Melissa seemed happier. She lifted her head, faced the trees and began to whistle. Joker was amazed. Melissa could whistle! He would never call her boring again. But why was she whistling? And how would it help Mia?

Joker gritted his teeth and paced up and down the garden, desperate to start searching for Mia.

'Patience, young soldier,' Rosco said. 'Save your energy for later. It's going to be a very long night.'

Within a few minutes, Joker's ears picked up a faint swishing sound. He looked up and his eyes widened as an owl flew into the garden. It circled once above the gathered animals and then landed in the cherry tree. Joker gaped at the bird. The tawny owl had brown speckled feathers and white spots on her wings, but what caught Joker's attention most were her magnificent eyes. Large and pitch black, they seemed to almost glow in the late afternoon sun. The owl folded her wings neatly and inspected the group below her.

'Greetings, Melissa. It has been a long time since you last called me.'

'Dearest Luna, thank you for coming.' Melissa bowed her head slightly. 'Many seasons have passed since we last met. I prefer a quiet life now.'

Joker's eyes darted from the owl to the cat and back again. Melissa had an owl friend. How extraordinary!

'What is the emergency?' Luna asked. 'You look worried.' The owl had a lovely, calm voice and Joker felt a bit better just hearing her talk.

Melissa told the owl about Mia and how she had ended up lost in the forest. Luna listened patiently and then focused her dark eyes on Joker.

'What does Mia look like?'

'She's about my size,' he answered. 'All black, except for her eyes. They're bright green.'

'Mmmhh, black cats are difficult to spot in the dark,' Luna said. 'But our main problem is the size of the forest. Mia could be anywhere.

I can fly and cover more ground than you, but that might still take too long. We don't have much time. If we want to save Mia, we'll have to find her before the foxes do.'

Joker jumped up and ran towards the gate. 'Yes, let's go,' he shouted. Finally, the waiting was over. He bounced on the spot, ready to rush into the forest, but Luna shook her head.

'No, Joker. We can't storm into the forest without a plan.' She looked at him kindly. 'I know you want to help your friend, but we must not panic.'

Joker pressed his lips together. What could they do? Where was Mia?

Luna closed her eyes and sat completely still. Joker sighed. He was getting more and more fidgety. After what felt like an eternity, the owl opened her eyes.

'We need to call the bats...'

Chapter 5

New Friends

Back in the forest, Mia woke up in the oak tree. She stretched her body and winced. It hurt to move. How long had she been asleep? The sun hung low in the sky and the light in the forest was fading. It must be early evening. At home, it would be time for food. Caroline and Steve would be worried. She needed to find her way back to them.

Had the dogs gone away? Mia climbed lower and searched the area. She couldn't see them anywhere. Maybe they were hiding nearby? She decided to wait a few more minutes. As she did so, she sniffed the air and listened hard for any unusual sounds. Suddenly, she saw movement in the ferns on the other side of the meadow. Something large and brown was coming towards her. She gasped and her ears flattened. Whatever she had seen seemed much bigger than a dog. Mia swallowed and her whiskers trembled as another fern moved slightly, this time a bit closer to her hiding place. If only she could make herself invisible. She held her breath. The forest was eerily quiet. Whatever was moving towards her was doing so very quietly.

And then she saw them. The animals were indeed bigger than dogs. They stopped from time to time to look around. There were two of them and they both had long ears, which were constantly twitching forwards, backwards and sidewards. At times, they pushed their noses high in the air as if they were trying to smell something.

Mia let out a big sigh of relief. Although the animals were bigger than dogs, she wasn't afraid anymore. They were deer, which meant they liked to eat grass and nibble at leaves, not hurt little kittens. Freddie had mentioned deer and some other animals that Mia might meet in the forest. He had warned her about foxes and eagles, as they might try to kill her, although he had also told her that most forest animals were friendly and helpful. Mia gathered all her courage and called to the nearest deer.

'Hello, can you help me?' She climbed to the lowest branch of the tree. 'I'm sorry to disturb you, but have you seen two big dogs? They chased me up here and I'm afraid to come down until I know they've gone.'

Both deer looked at Mia with their big brown eyes. The taller one answered.

'The dogs ran off a while ago. We watched them chase you. It's good to see that you managed to get away. My name is Dina, and my friend is called Dancer.' The deer had a kind voice and long curly eyelashes.

Mia smiled. 'I'm Mia,' she said. She told the deer about how she had moved to the new house with the big garden and explained that today was her first day in the forest.

'I was playing with my friend Freddie when the dogs attacked,' Mia said. 'I need to find my way home before it gets dark. I don't want to spend the night in the forest.'

Dina tilted her head and focused her large eyes on Mia. 'You poor thing, you've had quite an adventure today. You're too young to be here all alone.'

Mia climbed down the tree. 'Can you help me find my way back?'

Dina nodded. 'We can take you back to the fir trees where the dogs first found you. But you'll have to find your way home from there.'

'Thank you,' Mia said. The friendly deer would take her part of the way home, which was a good start at least. She felt a tiny flicker of hope. Maybe she would get home before it got dark? She took a step forward and winced.

Dina stopped and lowered her head. 'Does it hurt to walk?'

'A bit,' Mia admitted. 'The brambles had thorns and my pads hurt from all the running.'

Dina chuckled and lay down. 'Come on then, little Mia. You can ride on my back and rest.'

Mia's eyes lit up and her tail shot straight into the air. This was fantastic! She was going to hitch a ride on a deer. She climbed onto Dina's back.

'Hold tight,' Dina said as she stood up.

Mia slid forward and dug her claws in to keep her balance.

'Ouch, careful little panther.'

'I'm sorry, Dina.' Mia quickly pulled her claws back in. After a while, she got used to the movement of the deer. This was much better than walking. Dina's soft, warm fur made her feel safe. When she looked ahead, Mia noticed a crow in a nearby tree that stared at her. Was it the same crow she had seen earlier?

The deer carried Mia through the bracken and then through a large pine forest before coming to the bramble thicket. They walked around it and, a few minutes later, Mia recognised the big fir trees. She pointed to the moss where she had rested earlier. 'Stop, please. This is the place. I remember it.'

Mia jumped down from Dina's back and began to shout into the trees. 'Freddie! Freddie! Where are you?'

'Shush, little kitten. Quiet,' Dina said. 'You never know who might be listening.'

'But where is Freddie?' Mia asked, feeling tears well up in her eyes.

Dina sighed and gave Mia a nudge with her nose. 'Freddie searched long and hard for you, but he's gone now.'

'Freddie's gone?' Mia's head dropped and she swallowed hard. She would never find her way back home without Freddie.

Mia enjoyed riding on the deer

Dina cleared her throat. 'You need to be brave, little Mia.' The deer pointed her nose towards some hazelnut bushes. 'Freddie went that way, but you need to be careful. This is the time of day when foxes start to sneak around and look for their dinner.'

Dancer smiled reassuringly at her. 'Foxes can't climb very well. If you see a fox, quickly climb up the nearest tree and hide. And Mia, you will find your home, never stop believing that.'

Mia took a deep breath. Dancer was right. She would find her way back home. She would not give up. 'Thank you, Dina and Dancer. I will never forget your help. Joker won't believe me when I tell him that I rode on the back of a deer...'

CHAPTER 6

Mia Heads Home

After the deer left, Mia cast a nervous glance at the dark clouds above. She hoped it wouldn't rain. The cold wind ruffled her fur and she shivered. Leaves rustled while old wood creaked and groaned. Mia's eyes darted around. Her ears followed every strange noise. She was afraid of what might be lurking in the shadows. Her heart was beating way too fast. She took a few deep breaths to calm herself. Which way had she come that morning? She wasn't sure. The dim light made everything look different.

In the distance, she spotted a group of birch trees with pretty grey and white bark. Had she passed them that morning? She couldn't remember. If only she'd paid more attention. Her long tail seemed to have developed a life of its own and swished from side to side. It only took her a few minutes to reach the birches. She stopped. Nothing looked familiar. Mia's heart sank and she pressed her lips together, trying hard not to cry. She had no idea which direction to go in. She was lost in this horrible forest, and soon it would be dark.

Suddenly, she heard footsteps. She quickly climbed up the nearest tree. Once she was up high enough, she turned around and looked towards the forest floor far below. Who was coming towards her? She sniffed the air but didn't smell anything unusual. The rustling grew louder and Mia grew more afraid. When she finally saw what was making the noise, she dared to breathe again and even allowed herself a little smile.

Below her, a little hedgehog was running nimbly along the forest floor, nose in the leaves, foraging for things to eat. Maybe the hedgehog could help her?

'Hello!' she shouted.

The hedgehog quickly curled up and lay absolutely still. Mia climbed down and sat beside him. 'I'm not dangerous. I'm just a little kitten...' she whispered.

The prickly ball didn't move. Maybe the hedgehog couldn't hear very well?

'I'm lost,' Mia said a bit louder, keeping her eyes on the hedgehog's sharp spikes. Nothing. Not even a tiny flicker of movement. She took a deep breath and leaned as close as she dared. 'My name is Mia,' she called. 'Can you help me? Please!'

At first, nothing happened, but then the ball began to move. It rolled a little to one side and a small nose and two twinkly black eyes appeared. Mia sat still, not wanting to frighten the other animal. The hedgehog blinked a few times, sneezed and then slowly uncurled. He stood up, flattened his spikes and looked Mia up and down.

'Well, you gave me quite a fright, Miss Mia, shouting at me like that.' He bowed his head. 'Never mind. I'm Hugo. How can I help you, Miss Mia?'

Mia had seen hedgehogs before but never talked to one. His legs looked even shorter than her own. He seemed friendly.

'You shouldn't be here,' Hugo told her and shook his head. 'The forest is too dangerous for a kitten like you. You don't have the same protection that I do.' He used one of his front paws to point at his sharp spikes before brushing off some leaves.

Mia sighed. Her ears and long whiskers drooped. 'I know that now. Rosco and Melissa told me not to go into the forest, but I didn't listen... and now I'm lost and don't know where to go.' She felt tears coming and tried to blink them away.

'Please don't cry,' Hugo said. 'Why don't you tell me how you got here?'

Mia wiped a stray tear away before telling the little hedgehog the story of her day.

'Well, that's quite a tale,' he said when she had finished. 'Can you remember any of the places you saw this morning with Freddie?'

Mia chewed her lip, thinking hard. She remembered how much fun she'd had playing, but she hadn't paid much attention to anything else. She told the hedgehog about her house, the garden with the cherry tree and the metal gate in the fence. Unfortunately, Hugo had never seen the house or the garden. She remembered the hollow tree on the ground, but he didn't know that place either.

Mia frowned. 'I remember a stream and a pond with a strange-looking tree. We didn't stay long as I was chasing Freddie at the time.' She closed her eyes, trying to remember more details. 'I've never seen a tree like it before. It looked odd. It had long, thin branches that dangled almost to the ground.'

Hugo's ears pricked up. 'I know where you mean,' he said. 'Your strange tree is a willow tree, and there is only one in this forest.' His eyes sparkled and he chuckled. 'I knew you would remember something. Well done!'

Hugo smiled at her. 'It's a good walk, but I'll take you there. Follow me.'

Mia felt like a weight had been lifted off her shoulders. She was surprised at how quickly the hedgehog moved. She struggled to keep up with him. When they reached the willow tree half an hour later, she was limping badly. Every step hurt, but she gritted her teeth and plodded on. They sneaked under the hanging branches and rested near the big trunk.

'Thank you so much, Hugo,' Mia said. 'I must be much closer to my home now.' She groaned as she lay down to lick her sore paws.

The hedgehog cleared his throat. 'I hope you find your way back there,' he said in his kind voice. 'But do be careful and watch out, especially for foxes. They would love to eat you.'

Mia nodded, not trusting herself to say goodbye without starting to cry. The hedgehog winked at her and then hurried off into the forest. Mia sighed as she pondered what to do next. Everyone she had met had warned her about foxes. She would have to be careful. At least she was black, which meant it would be difficult for them to spot her in the dark.

She got up gingerly and hobbled to the stream. The cool water tasted delicious. She hadn't realised how thirsty she was after all the running and climbing. It was almost dark by the time she finished. A heavy raindrop hit her straight on the head, making her flinch. Angry clouds towered above her and thunder rumbled through the skies. Mia bit her lower lip and began to tremble. She didn't like this forest at all. At home, she would crawl under the sofa when she was scared. Where could she hide in this forest?

'Think, Mia! Don't give up,' she muttered to herself. She needed to find a safe place. The willow tree was not far from the stream. It would be a good place to hide, and the trunk had looked easy to climb. Tonight she would rest and then, in the morning, she would find her way back home.

Mia lifted her head and sniffed the air. Something smelled different. She didn't recognise the smell. It was quite strong and musty. Time to climb the tree, she thought as she squeezed underneath the branches of the large willow. The smell was much stronger under the tree. She lifted her head and gasped in shock. A red fox blocked her route to the trunk. He grinned at her, but not in a nice way.

'Well, well, well... I've been following you for a while,' he said.

Mia arched her back and puffed up her fur as much as possible, but she still felt tiny compared to the big fox.

'Quite clever, getting Dina and Hugo to help you, but I was never far away,' the fox hissed, showing off his sharp teeth. His mean eyes glowed orange as he took a step towards her. 'Do you know what my favourite food is?'

Mia swallowed and shook her head. She didn't want to know. Her heart hammered in her chest and her legs felt like jelly. Was this how she was going to die? She didn't want that to happen. What could she do?

The fox took his time. He licked his lips and gave Mia another evil smile before telling her about his favourite food.

'Kitten pie!' he shouted.

And then he jumped...

Chapter 7

The Fox

Fortunately, the fox had made a mistake. Mia had initially been so shocked that she just stood still as if glued to the ground with super strong glue. She couldn't move at all. If the fox had jumped straight away, she would have ended up as his dinner.

But while the fox was busy gloating about how clever he was, Mia had come up with a plan. She took a deep breath and pushed herself flat against the ground, pretending to cower in fear. Her only chance was to be brave and very fast. When the fox finally did jump, she was ready. She waited until he was in the air before throwing herself to one side. She ducked under the branches and raced towards the stream. If she could just reach the trees on the other side, she would be able to climb them. Then she would be safe.

The fox crashed through the branches behind her. He was close. Too close. She zigzagged towards the water. The stream looked huge but it was her only chance. Mia gritted her teeth and pushed off with her tiny legs. The next thing she knew, she was flying over the water...

It was a mighty jump and she almost made it. Her front paws touched the bank on the other side, but the leaves and grass were wet and slippery, and she couldn't hold on.

'Meow!' she cried as she slid down the bank and into the cold water. 'Help me!'

Mia couldn't touch the bottom with her feet and her head dropped under the water. She couldn't breathe and soon her lungs were burning. She kicked hard with all four legs, trying to get back to the surface. The stream carried her into a pond, where she finally managed to lift her head out of the water, gasping for air and coughing.

She kept paddling with her tired legs, but it was hard work. Through the rain, she spotted an island in the middle of the pond. Her eyes lit up. It didn't seem that far away. Maybe she could reach it?

Behind her, Mia heard the angry shouts of the fox. 'Come back, you silly kitten!'

Mia ignored the stupid fox. She would survive. She wouldn't listen to him. As she was getting closer to the island, the weather worsened and a vicious thunderstorm began. Raindrops clattered all around her and the gusty wind caused small waves in the pond, making swimming much harder. Mia swallowed a lot of water, her teeth chattered and she could feel herself weakening, but she forced her legs to keep moving.

Just when she felt that she couldn't paddle any longer, her feet touched solid ground. She dragged herself up the shore and collapsed in a quivering heap. For a few minutes, Mia just lay there, gasping for air and coughing up water, as the thunderstorm raged all around her. Flashes of lightning cut through the sky, followed quickly by loud bangs of thunder. Mia cowered on the island, trembling with fear. She had always hated thunder and lightning.

Once she had caught her breath, Mia staggered to her feet. She had made it. She shook herself and water drops sprayed everywhere.

Where was the fox? Mia squinted into the darkness but struggled to see anything through the heavy rain. A flash of lightning lit up the bank on the other side and she spotted him. He was pacing up and down. She looked at the expanse of water between them. It was a long way from the other shore to the island. Much too far to jump, even for a big fox.

Mia sat down and closed her eyes for a moment. She couldn't quite believe that she was still alive and had managed to escape. The fox couldn't get her, not unless he could swim. She chewed her upper lip, thinking. No, he would have followed her by now if he was able to swim. She smiled. She really was safe.

Mia turned around to have a closer look at the island. Apart from a few small bushes and one flimsy tree, it was bare. The tree was only small, probably not high enough to keep her safe if the fox did find a way to cross the water. She hoped he wasn't just pretending that he couldn't swim. Her whole body shivered and her teeth rattled loudly. She needed to get off the wet ground to dry out and get some rest.

The fox gloated

Mia began to climb the tree but struggled to get a grip of the damp bark. Twice she slid down before she managed to heave herself up the tree. She found a spot to curl up and closed her eyes, unable to keep them open any longer. The fox had still not given up. She could hear him shouting from far away.

'I'll find a way to get you. You're not safe there, you silly kitten.'

—

Back in Mia's garden, Luna the owl called into the forest.

'Hu, hu, hu—huuu, huuu, huuu—hu, hu, hu.'

'I know that code,' Rosco said. 'That's a distress signal, isn't it? Three short sounds, three long ones and then three short ones again.'

The owl nodded. 'The bats will know that someone needs help.' She turned to watch the forest. Joker was amazed to see how far Luna could turn her head without moving her body. He tried to copy her, but it hurt his neck and he almost fell over. Owls must have super flexible necks, he thought.

Seconds later, the first bat arrived, quickly followed by others. They whizzed around the garden so fast that Joker felt dizzy watching them. How did they manage not to fly into each other? Their wings looked different from Luna's. Instead of feathers, he saw thin skin stretched between lots of little bones. The bats could move their wings in many directions, not just up and down, and while there were some near misses, no one crashed.

After everyone had landed safely in the cherry tree, Joker realised that he had never seen so many bats before. He counted eleven. They had big ears, small eyes and rows of tiny teeth. Some were hanging upside down, whereas others were clinging to the trunk.

Luna waited until everyone had found a place before she began to talk. 'Thanks for coming. We need your help to find a black kitten who is lost in the forest. Her name is Mia.'

'Why should we help?' one of the bigger bats asked. 'Cats are our enemies.'

Joker frowned. Was that true? He quite liked bats. He thought they looked cute.

'I wouldn't hurt you,' he said.

Melissa stepped up beside him. 'I can't talk for all cats, but none of us will ever harm you.'

'We're pets,' Rosco added in his gruff voice. 'We're well fed and never hunt bats.'

Joker looked up at the bats and tilted his head. 'Please help us. Mia is my friend and she's all alone in the forest.'

The bats huddled together. Joker pressed his lips together and forced himself to sit still. Would they help? After a short time, a large bat with fluffy dark hair opened his mouth. He had a high-pitched voice and Joker had to strain his ears to hear what he said.

'My name is Kevin and I speak for all of us. We have come to a decision...' He paused. Joker held his breath. What had they decided? Kevin unfolded his wings and raised his head high. 'We will help you.'

'Hurrah!' Joker shouted as he somersaulted on the grass. He bounced around the garden like a crazy monkey dancing on hot lava. Everyone cheered and smiled. Even Rosco joined in, which didn't happen often. Luna asked Kevin to send the bats all over the forest and report back if they found any signs of Mia.

'Where will you be?' Kevin asked.

'I'll take the cats and the squirrel into the forest and we'll search for any tracks on the ground. We'll head to the hollow tree first.'

The bats flew off into the forest and fanned out in all directions. But the forest was big and Mia was small. Would they be able to find her in time?

Chapter 8

The Rescue

Joker watched the bats fly off. He cast a worried glance at the black clouds above. They looked angry, as if they were ready to burst. Gusts of wind blew leaves off the trees and thunder rumbled in the distance.

'Are we all ready?' Luna asked. Rosco stretched himself. Freddie jumped onto the back fence, tail all bushed up and twitchy. Joker gritted his teeth and nodded.

'How shall we do this?' Melissa asked.

Luna set out the plan. 'I'll fly ahead. Melissa, you lead the rest of the group. Keep Joker in the middle.'

Rosco moaned. 'Do we have to take him? He's too small. He'll get in the way.'

'I want to come.' Joker stood as tall as he could. 'Please.'

Luna focussed her big black eyes on him. 'Sometimes being small can be useful. We don't know what will happen tonight or who we might need. You can come, Joker.'

'Thank you, Luna,' Joker said. He was still scared but he wanted to help. He needed to help. After all, it was his fault that Mia was in danger.

By the time they were finally ready to leave the garden, the light had almost gone. Freddie shot up the nearest tree and Joker heard him jumping through the branches high above. Luna flew ahead. The three cats squeezed through the back gate and headed into the forest. Joker stayed close to Melissa. He could hear strange sounds everywhere. Leaves rustled and trees creaked. The damp air smelled of rotten wood and mushrooms. Joker sensed strange animals all around him, hidden in the darkness. When Rosco trod on a twig and caused it to loudly snap, Joker panicked and jumped forward. He bumped straight into Melissa's bottom.

'Sorry!' he shouted, jumping backwards and knocking into Rosco.

'Ouch! Be careful, you little devil,' Rosco complained.

'Shush,' Melissa hissed. 'Be quiet.' She threw them both a stern look. Rosco glared at Joker, who felt rather stupid and quickly looked away.

'Sorry, Rosco,' he whispered and flinched when a raindrop hit his nose. Soon after, the heavens opened and, within minutes, Joker was soaked to the skin. His ears pressed flat against his head and his tail swished from side to side. He hated getting wet.

Meeting at the hollow tree

'Follow me!' Melissa shouted over the noise of the storm. The three wet cats battled on through the wind and rain. Joker's heart threatened to stop every time a loud bang of thunder roared through the forest around him. He wished he could hide in his safe place under the stairs. He blinked away the water that ran into his eyes and focussed all his attention on Melissa's tail in front of him. He had to be brave. Mia was somewhere in this scary forest and she was all alone.

Luckily, the storm lasted only a short while. By the time they arrived at the hollow fallen tree, the rain had stopped. Freddie was already there, brushing his wet tail with his tiny paws. 'All clear here. No danger I can spot,' the squirrel said. 'But no sign of Mia. I hope the bats find her soon.'

Joker shook himself and water drops sprayed everywhere.

'Hey, careful!' Rosco grumbled. 'I'm wet enough, thank you very much.'

'Oops, sorry,' Joker said.

—

In a different part of the forest, far away from Joker and his friends, Hugo the hedgehog munched happily on a tasty earthworm. It had started to rain a few minutes earlier. He liked the rain because it helped him to unearth snails and earthworms, but he had never seen so many bats flying around during a storm. Why were they out flying in the rain? Hugo was curious. Hedgehogs are generally very nosy, and he was no exception. He watched as another bat flew by. It looked like it was searching for something. What was going on?

'Hello there, night pilot!' Hugo called. 'What is it you are looking for?'

The bat whizzed around and landed close to Hugo on a small twig. It folded its large wings and looked at the hedgehog through tiny black eyes. Hugo knew that bats could fly even when it was dark, but he had often wondered how they did so without crashing into trees. He was a bit jealous. It would be cool to be able to fly, and so much quicker.

'Hello, my prickly friend,' the bat said. 'I'm looking for a black kitten.'

Hugo's head shot up. 'A kitten? I saw a black one earlier,' he said. 'I felt sorry for the poor little thing. She was lost and scared. She said her name was Mia.'

The bat's big ears swivelled towards Hugo. 'Where did you see her?' he asked in a squeaky voice.

'I showed her the way to the stream, near the big willow tree. You must know the place. The stream flows into a large pond.'

'Yes, I know exactly where that is. It's a great place for catching insects above the water. Thank you so much. I'll call the others and we can focus our search there. Hopefully we'll find her before she gets into too much trouble.'

Within minutes, Hugo was surrounded by bats. They all landed nearby, water dripping off their thin black wings.

'Wow, spooky. How did you call them?'

Kevin the bat looked smug. 'That, my new hedgehog friend, is a secret. You can call it our superpower. It's a useful tool at times like this. We can call each other and no one else can hear us. I told the others where you last saw Mia, so now we'll search there.'

Hugo was surrounded by bats

Kevin unfolded his wings and, fast as the wind, disappeared with his bat friends into the night. Hugo hoped they would find Mia in time.

Freddie, Joker, Melissa and Rosco were waiting by the hollow tree. The rainclouds had blown away and the Moon provided a bit of light. Joker kept thinking about Mia. What if the bats couldn't find her?

He was relieved, when he heard the familiar swishing of big wings and Luna appeared. The tawny owl landed neatly on the fallen tree and flapped her wings a few times, shaking off a lot of water.

'Good news,' she said. 'We've got a clue as to where Mia might be.' She told them what Kevin had learned from Hugo and explained that the bats were now searching the area near the pond and the willow tree.

'I know where that is,' Rosco said. 'We used to play there when we were younger. Do you remember, Melissa?'

'I certainly do. You used to chase me up that willow tree,' she said and began to giggle. Joker's lower jaw dropped. He couldn't imagine the two older cats chasing each other.

'Don't look so surprised, young man,' Rosco said. 'We were young once and used to get into all sorts of trouble.'

'Let's not waste any time chatting,' Luna said. 'We haven't found Mia yet. I'll fly ahead and we'll meet by the willow tree.'

Melissa set off at a trot, Joker and Rosco following behind. Freddie hurtled through the branches above. Melissa had not lied. She did know the way to the willow. Joker lost all sense of direction as they ran across the forest floor.

First, they ran through pine trees. The brown needles felt soft under his paws and following Melissa was easy. The trouble started when they reached a thicket of brambles. Melissa wiggled through. Joker followed closely behind her, too close as it turned out. Twice, thorny brambles whipped into his face. It didn't help that he was starting to get tired. His paws hurt and he was breathing heavily. He needed a rest, but Melissa kept running. They jumped over a small stream and pushed through some nettles on the other side. The nettles stung Joker's skin and he winced in pain. Suddenly, Melissa stopped and Joker almost bumped into her bottom for the second time that night. He slid to a standstill, gasping for breath.

'What's going on?' Rosco asked from behind.

'Wait here,' Melissa hissed.

Joker watched as the older cat scouted ahead. He frowned. Why were they stopping? Melissa dashed back and glanced at the nearest tree.

'Do you want us to climb up?' Rosco whispered.

Melissa nodded and rushed up the tree at a speed that impressed Joker. He scampered after her, followed by Rosco. They settled on a thick branch a few metres above the forest floor and watched the path below. Soon, they heard footsteps. Someone was coming!

Joker spotted the foxes first. They trotted towards them, side by side, their mouths hanging slightly open. The moonlight shone on their white and very sharp-looking teeth. The two foxes stopped directly underneath the tree. Joker's eyes bulged with fear and he began to tremble.

'I can smell cat,' the bigger of the two foxes said, moving his head from side to side and sniffing the air.

The smaller fox nodded. 'Yes, I can smell it too. Must be close by.'

Joker bit his lip. His breathing sounded too loud. Would the foxes be able to hear it? They kept sniffing the air and peering into the woods, ears pricked. Joker watched them wide-eyed, desperately hoping they wouldn't look up.

'All quiet,' the big fox said after a while, 'although I can still smell cat.'

'Master, maybe you can still smell the kitten that got away?'

The big fox growled and sank his teeth into the leg of the smaller fox.

'Ouch!' the little fox screamed in pain.

'Keep your stupid mouth shut or it will hurt a lot more next time.'

Joker thought about what he had just heard. Mia was alive. That was good news. He smiled. Mia had somehow managed to escape this big bully. But Joker's heart almost jumped out of his chest when he heard what the fox said next...

'Let's go back to the pond and see if we can get onto the island. I fancy a bit of sweet kitten meat for breakfast.' He laughed, but it was a nasty laugh and Joker felt the fur on his back rising.

'Whatever you say, Master,' the smaller fox whimpered. He limped after the bigger fox, keeping his head low.

The cats watched as the foxes turned around and disappeared into the forest. Joker's chest felt tight and he had a sour taste in his mouth. He looked at his companions, unable to speak. Mia was alive, but she was still in great danger.

Not one but two foxes were coming for her.

Chapter 9

The Island

Mia woke up confused. She had dreamed of her soft bed and food, lots of lovely food. Where was she? Why was she on top of a tree? Her eyes widened as she remembered. The fox had almost caught her last night. She had escaped to the island, but now she was stuck. Her head dropped and she sighed heavily. Would she ever get back home? She whimpered in pain. Everything hurt. She began licking her wounds but stopped when she saw several bats approaching. The biggest bat landed on a branch nearby. Mia thought it looked cute.

'Hi Mia, I'm Kevin,' the bat said in a high-pitched, slightly squeaky voice. 'We've been searching for you for a long time. You were hidden well in this tree.'

Mia couldn't believe her ears. 'Why were you looking for me?'

'You have friends, Mia. They're all out looking for you.' Kevin shook his head. 'It was a stupid thing to do, to go into the forest by yourself. You could have died.'

Mia lowered her eyes. 'I know. I should have listened to Rosco and Melissa. I got into all sorts of trouble last night and couldn't find my way home.' She felt tears welling up again. 'I don't even know in which direction to search next if I'm ever going to find a way off this island.'

'Mia, stop crying. Please!' Kevin said. 'Why do you think we've searched all night? We want to help you.'

Mia sniffed and lifted her head. 'Really? You'll help me?' she asked and felt a tiny bit of hope begin to build. Maybe all was not lost. Kevin told her that Luna the owl was supervising the search and that Freddie, Rosco, Melissa and Joker were somewhere in the forest looking for her. Mia struggled to take it all in. She wasn't alone?

'I'll let the others know where you are,' Kevin said. 'Don't move from this spot until help arrives. The foxes are still sneaking around. Stay here!'

Mia nodded. She would listen this time and wait for her friends. Besides, she was trapped on the island anyway. Kevin unfolded his wings and flew away. Mia yawned and curled up into a little ball. She shivered in the cold morning air and hoped that her friends would arrive soon.

—

Back in the forest, Melissa, Rosco and Joker tracked the two foxes. They followed at a safe distance, hiding behind trees and bushes. Joker's tail was all bushed up and his ears swivelled in all directions. He could smell the foxes, and his whiskers twitched nervously.

Melissa had sent the squirrel ahead. 'The foxes want to kill Mia. You need to warn Luna. We might not have much time.'

The foxes were still talking to each other and had no idea that they were being followed.

'I'm tired and my leg hurts,' the smaller fox moaned. 'I want to go home.'

'We're not going home,' the bigger fox said. 'I know how we can get onto the island and get our kitten breakfast.'

The foxes picked up their speed and raced ahead.

'Run faster!' Rosco shouted. 'We have to keep up with them. Maybe we can distract them at the pond?'

Melissa nodded grimly and the three cats sprinted after the foxes. Joker tried his best to keep pace with the older cats, which was not easy as his legs were a lot shorter.

—

In a different part of the forest, Kevin had found Luna. 'I've told Mia to stay on the island and wait for help. But we have a problem.' The bat scratched his head. 'I'm not sure how we can get Mia off the island. She's cold and weak.'

'Is she safe where she is at the moment?' Luna asked.

'The tree is not tall. A fox could probably jump that high, but I don't think any fox could get to the island. It's too far to jump across, even for a big fox.'

'That's good news. We should have a bit of time to come up with a plan then. Let me think.'

Luna sat still, eyes closed. After a few minutes, she opened her eyes. 'Kevin, I have two more jobs for you and the other bats. First, find Dina the deer and ask her to come to the pond. Second, I want you to get all the other animals together. Tell them to stay hidden near the pond, so the foxes won't see them.' Luna carried on talking, explaining her plan in more detail. Kevin listened carefully.

'Everyone has to wait for my signal. Whatever happens,' she said after she finished explaining.

Kevin nodded and then flew into the forest. The bats would be busy for a bit longer that morning.

—

Back on the little island, Mia lifted her head and listened. She had heard something. There it was again. The sound was coming from the forest. She heard twigs breaking. When she looked across the pond, she spotted the fox and instantly felt the hairs on her back rising. He was not alone this time. He was accompanied by a smaller darker coloured fox. She watched the two foxes carefully. The bigger one was clearly the leader. He walked towards the stream that fed into the pond. The smaller fox followed, limping. What were they doing?

The foxes seemed to be searching for something near the water's edge. Suddenly, the bigger fox laughed. He had a horrible, nasty laugh that made Mia tremble. She heard him talking to the other fox.

'Help me move this.'

Mia looked more closely and gasped in shock as she realised what the foxes were doing. She watched in horror as they freed a big branch that had been lying on the shore, halfway in the water. They managed to roll it fully into the water and push it towards the island.

Mia's heart was racing so fast that it hurt her chest and her legs were shaking. What could she do? The bats had vanished. She was all alone. There was no sign of her friends or the mysterious owl that Kevin had talked about. They had probably seen the foxes and abandoned their rescue mission. After all, what could they do against two foxes? Mia looked at her little tree and sighed. She could climb a bit higher and cling to one of the upper branches, but she feared it would not be high enough to keep her out of reach of the foxes.

'Careful now, don't rush,' she heard the bigger fox calling. The foxes were holding on to one end of the branch with their teeth and front paws as the current moved the other end towards the island. Soon it would hit the shore. Then the foxes would have a perfect bridge and could stroll over to the island. Mia knew that she would not stand a chance in her flimsy tree against two foxes.

'Hey, little kitty. Guess who's coming?'

Mia's heart beat so loud, it rang in her ears. What could she do?

'Nobody outfoxes me,' the big fox growled, his fierce eyes glaring at her. 'You could have saved us a lot of time and trouble by giving in.'

Mia watched the two foxes

Why was he so mean? Mia hated him. She watched helplessly as the two foxes gave the log one last push.

Chapter 10

Foxes and Friends

Joker's whiskers twitched. As usual, he found it difficult to sit still. He could just about see Luna, who was sitting on top of the big willow tree. The owl had tried to reassure everyone about her plan, but Joker was still worried. Would it work? He sneaked forward a bit. He couldn't see the foxes anymore. Where were they? Rosco was blocking his view. The cats had positioned themselves in trees next to the pond. While Melissa sat in the next tree, her eyes fixed on the foxes and Luna, Joker was sharing his branch with Rosco.

'Be careful, Joker. Don't push me off,' Rosco whispered.

Melissa glared at both of them. Joker sighed in frustration and looked around. Freddie winked at him from his hiding spot higher up in the tree. The squirrel had brought some friends to come and help. All the squirrels were holding nuts, acorns and even stones in their little paws. Hugo the hedgehog hid on the forest floor behind a big tree trunk and Joker had seen two more hedgehogs nearby. The bats were more difficult to spot, but he had counted at least twenty. He looked over to the island and saw Mia clinging to the top branch of a flimsy-looking tree. She had spotted the two foxes and Joker could tell that she was terrified.

His heart went out to Mia. He still felt guilty. He should have warned her about the dangers of the forest. How he wished he could tell her that she was not alone and that help was close by, but the owl had forbidden any contact with Mia before the signal.

Joker spotted the big branch around the same time as the foxes. He watched as they rolled it into the water and started pushing it towards the island. His heart sank as he realised that Mia had no chance of escape.

'Be careful, you idiot! You have to keep it still,' the bigger fox grumbled as he placed his front paws on the branch. It wobbled and he struggled to keep his balance on the slippery wood.

'I don't want to fall in,' he moaned. The branch was just a bit too short to fully reach the island. He moved all four paws onto the log and then tried to get his balance.

Joker watched wide-eyed. What was the owl waiting for?

'Come on, Luna,' he whispered.

'You're almost there, Master. Just one little jump.' The smaller fox was holding on to one end of the branch with his front paws. Suddenly, an owl hooted from the willow tree.

'Huuuhh, Huuuhh.'

Not once but twice. The sound echoed through the forest.

'Did you hear that, Master?'

'Careful, you idiot!' the big fox shouted as the branch bobbed in the water.

'Sorry, Master.'

Neither of the foxes noticed that the owl had left the willow tree and was now flying towards them. Joker tensed all his muscles and crouched low. The hooting had been the first signal for everyone to get ready. Luna flying towards the foxes was the final signal that everyone had waited for it, more or less patiently.

Finally, the wait was over. Joker jumped out of the trees before anyone else. He was scared but he wanted to help Mia. For the plan to work, they all needed to play their part. He ran towards the smaller fox and aimed for his tail. Melissa and Rosco caught up with him and reached the fox at the same time. The older cats grabbed the fox's hind legs with their teeth just as Joker jumped up and bit the tail.

'Ouch!' the little fox screamed and let go of the big branch.

The squirrels pelted him with nuts and stones. Some hit his head, others his belly.

'Ouch, ouch, ouch,' he cried and ran off as fast as his legs would carry him.

The bigger fox was in even more trouble.

'Don't leave me here, you fool!' he shouted, just about managing to keep his balance on the branch. He crouched ready for his final jump onto the island, but he had not reckoned with Luna. The owl gathered speed and swooped down towards the water. She stretched out her legs and smashed into the fox's side, digging her sharp talons deep into his skin.

The fox had no chance against Luna. He landed in the water with a big splash. The old branch broke into several pieces. The animals cheered, not noticing that the fox managed to get back onto the bank quickly. He was bleeding, but looked furious.

Joker was the first to realise that the fight was not over yet. 'Attack!' he shouted, all fear forgotten. He could sense Melissa and Rosco just behind him. The other animals reacted quickly and joined the cats' attack. The sky was filled with bats, Luna swooping amongst them. The squirrels reloaded and a few of the nuts and stones they threw found their target. The fox looked terrified. He turned and ran away with his tail between his legs, moving faster than Joker thought possible.

'Hurrah!' Joker shouted. All the animals cheered and laughed.

'He'll be sore for a few days,' Rosco said grimly.

The whole attack had lasted only a few minutes. It was quiet afterwards, as most of the animals were catching their breath.

Luna swooped down towards the fox

Luna flew over to Mia. 'Hello, Mia. Nice to finally meet you.'

'I thought I was going to die,' Mia said. 'The fox was so close. I could smell his awful breath.' She shuddered but still managed to smile weakly at the owl. 'Thank you so much! You all saved my life.'

Joker ran to the shore and shouted across. 'Hi, Mia! I'm so glad you're safe!'

He bounced on the spot and Mia saw that his eyes were sparkling. She smiled back as she heard Melissa's voice.

'Mia is still trapped. How is she going to get off that island?'

'Good point,' Rosco muttered.

Everyone stopped smiling. Melissa was right. Mia was still in trouble. How was she going to get off the island?

Chapter 11

Teamwork

The group's mood changed instantly. The foxes were gone, but a huge problem remained. How could they get Mia off the island?

'Can you swim, Mia?' Kevin asked. 'It's not very far and you did manage to paddle to the island last night.'

Mia shook her head. 'I was lucky last night and even then I almost drowned.' She looked at the water and a few tears dropped onto her cheek. She gingerly walked to the water's edge and dipped one paw into the water. It was cold, just as she remembered.

'Stop, Mia! Don't try to swim,' Melissa said. 'Give us a bit of time. Together we'll find a better solution.'

Mia sat down. She was exhausted and scared of the water, but what other option was there? She was too weak to swim and she couldn't fly. It was hopeless. She was going to have to either die on the island or drown trying to leave it.

'We could build a bridge,' Luna suggested. 'We just need another long piece of wood.'

'Yeah, great idea,' Freddie agreed eagerly.

All the animals fanned out to search for a suitable piece of wood. The big branch that the foxes had tried to use earlier must have been rotten as it had broken into several pieces when Luna hit the large fox. The squirrels finally found a long branch. Together, the animals managed to drag it to the pond and push it towards the island. It just about reached the other shore and Freddie was getting excited. He was jumping around, his tail all bushed up.

He shouted, 'Look, we've got a bridge.'

'It looks a bit flimsy,' Melissa said, but Mia felt a tiny glimmer of hope starting to build inside her. Could this be her escape route?

'I don't think that branch is big enough to support Mia's weight,' Luna warned.

'It's big enough. Trust me,' Freddie said. 'Look, I'll show you.'

The tiny squirrel jumped onto the branch, which instantly disappeared into the water, taking Freddie with it. He shrieked in panic and splashed around in the water. Rosco reacted quickly and scooped him out. Freddie was soaking wet but otherwise unharmed.

Mia dropped her head and her shoulders sagged. Her friends were close but she couldn't reach them.

'There might be another way,' Luna said.

Mia's ears pricked up and she lifted her head. The owl cleared her throat before continuing to talk. 'A bridge would have been perfect, but it didn't work. We now have no choice but to try the fallback plan.'

Mia's jaw dropped. There was another plan?

'What is this fallback plan?' Melissa asked with raised eyebrows. She was not the only one who was curious. All the animals looked at the tawny owl.

'Well, it's more of an idea really,' the owl admitted. 'It depends on two things. First, it will only work if the pond is not too deep and, second, we need to rely on the kindness of another friend.

Joker looked puzzled. Why did it matter how deep the pond was? And who was this other friend Luna was talking about? Only Kevin seemed to understand.

The bat said, 'We'll soon know. She should be here any minute now.'

Just as Kevin finished talking, the overhanging branches of the willow tree were pushed aside and two deer stepped into the clearing.

'Dina. It's you!' Mia shouted.

Dina bowed her head. 'Kevin asked me to come. He said that you were in a bit of bother and that I might be able to help. I see what he meant now. You're stuck there, aren't you?'

Mia nodded miserably. She liked Dina, but how could a deer help her? Deer could not fly.

Joker could not take his eyes off the deer. Dina had huge brown eyes and long eyelashes and she talked in a gentle, kind voice. There was another deer with her, staying a bit behind.

Dina walked closer and approached Luna. 'Kevin said to hurry and you would explain your plan once we got here...'

Luna addressed the deer respectfully. 'Thank you for coming, Dina.'

The owl hesitated briefly before explaining her idea. 'You should be able to wade over to the island. The water doesn't look very deep. Mia told me that you let her ride on your back yesterday. This will be similar, only in the pond.'

Dina walked to the shore and stared into the green water. 'Well, there's only one way to find out how deep it is.' She turned around and looked at her companion. 'Are you willing to help, Dancer? '

'Yes, of course,' the second deer answered as he stepped closer. 'I don't mind getting wet, provided I can touch the bottom of the pond.'

'Be careful, Dina.' Mia said.

Dina carefully placed first one and then the other front foot into the pond. Initially, it didn't look very deep, but as she stepped forward it got deeper quickly and soon only her head was showing above the water. That wasn't good news. The pond was deeper than Luna had expected.

Mia could barely watch. 'Please be careful, Dina.'

'I'll be fine, Mia.' Dina managed to say. 'Dancer, get in the water behind me.'

The deer arrived to help

'Remember to keep your head up as high as you can.'

Dancer quickly stepped into the pond. 'Don't worry, Mia. We will get you off that island.'

Joker held his breath. Would the deer manage to get to Mia? All eyes were glued to the pond and the deer. Would Dina try to swim the final bit? She was still a good distance away from the island.

But Dina had other plans. 'Mia, I know you're brave and I know you can jump well.'

Mia nodded. She could jump well.

'I cannot come any closer,' Dina said. 'But you can use our heads as landing spots and jump across to the other shore.'

Mia looked across the water into Dina's eyes. 'I'm not sure I can jump that far,' she said quietly.

Joker shouted across the pond, 'You can do it, Mia! You're a good jumper!'

Mia bit her lip. She was cold and unsure if she had enough strength left to make the necessary jumps. She looked across the pond. All of the animals were watching her. She sighed as she realised that it was the only way. To get off the island, she needed to find enough courage and strength to jump onto the heads of her new deer friends. If she slipped or misjudged a jump, she would be in trouble.

Chapter 12

The Jump

Melissa urged the other animals to stand back from the shore. 'Mia will need space. Come on everyone, move.'

The animals all shuffled a few feet back without taking their eyes off Mia and the deer. Mia kept thinking about the deep water. Her legs were shaking and she couldn't breathe properly. Dina's head looked awfully far away. She didn't think she could jump that far.

'Mia, calm down!' Dina said. 'Take a few deep breaths. Close your eyes and imagine the first jump. You can do this, but you need to be brave.'

Mia swallowed. 'I want to, but I'm scared that I'll fall into the water.' She sighed and her ears and whiskers drooped. Joker could see how terrified Mia was. No wonder, he thought. She had almost drowned yesterday. Maybe he could help?

'Mia, look at me!' he said gently. 'I know you. You're an excellent jumper. Come on, you can do this!'

Mia lifted her head and looked over at Joker. He had been very brave to attack the fox. He was her friend and he believed that she could do it. She swallowed and took a deep breath.

'I'm getting a bit cold here,' Dancer said. She could hear the deer's teeth chattering.

'Sorry, Dancer,' Mia said and stretched her body. 'I'm ready now.'

Luckily, her legs had stopped shaking and she was breathing more normally now. All of her friends thought she could do it, so she would give it her best shot. There was no other way. Mia took a few steps back and narrowed her eyes. She took one more deep breath and focussed all her attention on Dina's head, which was sticking out of the water about two metres away. Mia ignored her aching legs, sprinted to the shore and jumped towards the deer's head. Dina kept her eyes closed the whole time. Mia landed on top of the deer's head, right between her two big ears.

Dancer's head was a further two metres away. Mia did not pause. She jumped again quickly and reached the second deer's head. One of her back paws slipped and ended up on Dancer's nose. Mia's heart skipped a beat. She did not want to fall into the water. She hurled herself forward, putting all her remaining strength into the final jump. She was so close to safety. Joker could barely watch.

Mia flew through the sky, but soon realised that she hadn't jumped quite far enough.

'Argh!' she screamed.

A second later, she hit the cold water and sank like a stone. When she tried to breathe, she swallowed water instead. Her chest was hurting badly. She desperately needed air. Her feet touched something firm. Before she had time to react, she was propelled upwards and flew through the air. She landed on the bank with a big thud.

'Ouch!' she cried and then everything went black.

Joker was by her side in an instant. He had watched as Dancer had lowered his head deep into the water and pushed Mia out using his nose. Was she alive? She had not moved since she hit the ground. Joker almost jumped out of his skin when Mia suddenly gasped for air. Then she coughed up a lot of water. She was alive! He started to lick her face frantically.

'I'm alright, Joker,' Mia managed to say after a few more coughs.

Mia landed on the deer's head

She felt a bit dizzy and it hurt to breathe, but she was happy to be on dry land. She gingerly got up and shook herself, showering everyone nearby with cold water. Joker laughed. Mia was safe. Nothing else mattered as far as he was concerned.

Some of the others were not as pleased about getting a soaking. 'Stop it. I'm getting all wet,' Rosco moaned, although he smiled at the same time.

Melissa gave Mia a nudge with her nose. 'Promise never to go into the forest by yourself again.'

'I promise.' Mia looked at her friends. They were all still there, although some of the bats had started yawning.

Luna spoke next. 'All of us played our part last night. Without you bats, we would not have found Mia in time.'

The bats sat up a bit straighter and smiled proudly. Luna turned towards the deer. 'Dina and Dancer helped Mia after the dogs had attacked her and again later to get her off the island.' The owl tilted her head towards the hedgehogs and the squirrels.

'Hugo showed Mia the way to the willow tree while Freddie alerted the cats and got the other squirrels to help fight the foxes.'

Freddie's tail was swishing wildly as he jumped from branch to branch.

The owl raised her voice. 'None of us could have saved Mia on our own. By working together, we were so much stronger. We even scared away two foxes!'

Everyone cheered loudly and many animals clapped or hooted. Joker did a somersault and the bats showed off their flying skills.

Mia felt dizzy as she watched them whizzing through the air. She still struggled to believe that she was finally safe. She looked at her friends.

'I'll always remember what you did for me. I would have died without your help. It was stupid to go into the forest by myself, but I didn't think it would be dangerous. I just wanted an adventure.'

'You got your adventure all right,' Joker said.

'I got a lot more adventure than I ever wanted. I was so scared most of the time. You all risked a lot to save me and I will never forget that. I know I'm only a small kitten but I will grow bigger and, if any of you ever need help, find me and I will help you if I can.'

'Well spoken,' Luna said. 'We all make mistakes. That is life. The trick is to learn from each mistake and not to make the same one twice.'

'Time for us to retire,' Kevin said and Mia watched as the bats flew off into the forest.

Luna tilted her head. 'I've got a feeling we'll meet again, little Mia.'

Mia squinted into the sunlight as the tawny owl spread her wings and disappeared among the trees. The sky was blue. It looked like it was going to be a lovely day.

'I'll head back too,' Hugo said. 'It's time for my morning nap.'

'Thank you, Hugo,' Mia said as the hedgehog bowed his head before running off towards the willow tree.

Freddie hugged Mia. 'I'll visit soon. We can play again, once you've recovered.'

Mia felt her eyes welling up with tears, tears of joy this time. She was safe and she had made so many new friends. The squirrels lined up and all gave one last salute before scurrying away into the trees. The only animals left were the four cats and the deer.

'Time to get you home,' Rosco declared.

Dina stepped forward. 'It's still a good walk from here to your garden. We would be happy to give you another ride. You look exhausted.'

Joker's ears pricked up. Dancer smiled encouragingly at Mia. 'Don't get used to it. When you're well, you'll have to walk.'

'Oh, I hoped I could have a go as well,' Joker said. His whiskers and ears drooped. He had so looked forward to riding on a deer. Dancer laughed and lay down. 'Well, hop on then. Let's get you home.'

Melissa and Rosco refused to ride on the deer. They ran ahead to show the way. Mia rode Dina and Joker sat on Dancer. It was a bit wobbly, but after a few steps Joker relaxed and enjoyed it. The deer's hair was soft and warm. He looked to his side and smiled at Mia, his new best friend.

'Mia, I'm glad you're safe. I was so worried about you.'

Mia smiled back. 'I still can't believe it. I saw you jumping out of the trees ahead of everyone. You were really brave. Thank you, Joker!'

If cats could blush, Joker would have turned bright red. He grinned and his eyes sparkled. 'I just jumped faster than the others. I never meant to be at the front.'

'It was still very brave to attack the fox, Joker. You truly are a good friend to be willing to risk so much for me.'

Joker felt happy, happier even than the day he'd found the dish of clotted cream on the coffee table and he had been pretty happy then. The ride was over too quickly as far as he was concerned. Riding on a deer certainly was a great way to travel.

'We'll have to leave you now,' Dina said. Mia jumped down and winced. Her bruises and scratches were hurting.

'Thank you, Dina,' she said. 'You have been such a good friend. I don't know how I'll ever repay you.'

'Who knows what the future will bring? There might come a time when I need your help.'

Joker weaved around Dancer's legs. The deer seemed to have taken a shine to the tabby kitten.

'See you again sometime, little soldier,' Dancer said. Then both deer turned around and trotted back into the forest.

Rosco looked at the two kittens. 'Melissa and I have decided to start teaching you...'

'Really? Like school?' Mia said.

'Well, a bit like school,' Rosco said. 'Someone needs to keep an eye on you pair. You seem to have quite a talent for getting into trouble.'

They were interrupted by Caroline's voice calling from the garden. 'Mia, come home. Food's ready.'

Steve joined in. 'Mia, sweety. Where are you?'

Both of Mia's owners had been up all night searching for her.

Steve was the first to see the cats. He dropped the can of food he was holding. 'Look, Caroline! They're all together.'

Caroline started to cry. 'Mia, you're safe! I thought we'd lost you.'

Steve spotted Mia first

'I think our little kitten has made some new friends,' Steve said. 'I'd love to know what happened to them last night.'

'That we'll never know, but at least she's back.' Caroline wiped away some tears and sniffed happily. Steve picked Mia up and carried her into the house.

Mia was pleased to be back in Steve's arms and began to purr. Her tummy was grumbling. She was looking forward to food, lots of food, and then to a long sleep in the soft bed upstairs. She could barely keep her eyes open. Attending kitten school and playing with her new friends would have to wait for another day.

The End

Mia could barely keep her eyes open

Dear reader,

I hope you enjoyed reading *Mia is Lost* as much I loved writing it.

Next time, you go into the woods, look out for the different forest animals. Maybe you can spot Freddie the squirrel eating a hazelnut or Hugo the hedgehog munching on an earthworm. And if you are really lucky you might get a glimpse of Dina the deer or Luna the tawny owl.

Try to find at least three different trees. Oak, pine and birch trees should be quite easy to spot but can you find a weeping willow?

If you want to learn more about the different forest animals or do some fun activities, then visit Mia's website **www.jkkeane.co.uk.**

There you can see cute photos of real life Mias or mini black panthers as I call them. Black cats are sadly often overlooked and struggle more than their colourful friends to find forever homes. So if you visit a rescue or shelter, please remember little Mia and don't walk by...

If you feel a bit sad that you have reached the end of the book, don't worry — Mia's adventures have barely started. In the next book, *Mia Fights Back*, Mia and Joker will go to forest school, meet new friends, but also have to fight to save one of the other forest animals.

If you enjoyed this book, please tell your friends, your teachers and other parents or grandparents about it so that they can read it as well. Thank you.

I hope, you follow Mia and her friends on her new adventures.

JK Keane

For a sneaky preview read on....

Extract of *Mia Fights Back* due to be published in the summer of 2023.

When Mia heard the key in the front door, she swallowed once but didn't move from her position in front of the locked cat flap. She clenched her jaw, lifted her chin, and tried to ignore her racing heart. Until her humans accepted that she wasn't a housecat, there would be war.

Seconds later, they stormed into the kitchen. Steve carried several letters, or more precisely what was left of them.

'Mia, you little devil. This has to stop.'

Mia's whiskers twitched as she tried not to smile. Chewing the letters had been good fun.

Steve's face turned bright red when he saw the state of the kitchen. Caroline opened her mouth and dropped to her knees. 'Mia, what have you done?'

Mia bit her lip. Truth be told, she felt a bit guilty. She had pushed over the water bowl, pulled two plant pots from the windowsill and had shredded the kitchen roll. The water and brown earth had mixed well. Muddy cat footprints covered the white tiles and continued onto the beige carpet in the conservatory, leading to the shut cat flap. Just in case her owners didn't get the message she had also scratched the new carpet in the hallway. No wonder they were upset. But it was their own fault. Why did they keep her locked up? She would be nice again as soon as they let her out.

'Look at her, sitting there by the cat flap. That kitten is a monster,' Steve grumbled.

Caroline walked over and stroked Mia's head. 'Why can't you be a housecat? Don't you remember what happened last time?'

Mia pressed her lips together but didn't move. She did remember. She had spent a whole night on her own, lost in the nearby forest. Without the help of the neighbourhood cats and some of the forest animals, she would have died that night. The foxes would have killed her. Mia knew she still had a lot to learn. The older cats had promised to start a kitten school and she was looking forward to it. But first, she needed to persuade her humans to let her out.

Steve tiptoed around the obstacles on the floor towards her. Mia held her breath. Would he finally open the cat flap? Would Caroline allow it?

'She's too wild to be locked inside forever. All her cuts and bruises have healed,' Steve said. 'We need to let her out.' Mia's heart skipped a beat.

Caroline nodded. 'Be careful, Mia,' she said. 'No more silly adventures, please.'

Steve glanced through the window into the garden. 'The neighbour's kitten is outside again. He hangs around a lot. I wonder if he fancies our Mia.'

Mia's eyes lit up. Joker was waiting for her. Great! Unable to sit still any longer, she bounced up and down, almost bursting with excitement. Soon she would explode. Steve bent down and moved the latch that locked the catflap.

'Go on, you rascal, get out,' he said with a smile on his face.

Acknowledgments

Do you remember the quote at the beginning of this book?

Here it is again, in case you forgot.

"Alone we can do so little; together we can do so much." - Hellen Keller -

Rescuing Mia worked because the animals worked together as a team. Writing and publishing a book is also a great team effort. I owe a massive thanks to so many people, who helped me during the last three years to move from a story idea to a finished book that children and their parents can read and hopefully enjoy.

A big thank you goes to Helen Brain, who tutored me through two separate creative writing courses at the Writers College and taught me so much.

The best advice I ever got was to join a writing group. Thanks to Mirel and James from the Skywriters who critiqued my first draft and encouraged me to keep writing.

A huge thank you to all my writing buddies at the Writers on the Edge. Without you this book would never have been published. Getting feedback from so many talented writers and being able to discuss writing issues and reading other people's work has really helped me. Thank you to Alison, Anne, Brenda, Charles, Denise, Gillian, Kathy, Laurelle, Sara and Tom for the warm welcome, the encouragement, the cakes and for forcing me to read my stories out loud.

A special thanks must go to Jo Jackson and Maggie Bardsley. I owe you a lot! Thank you for your advice, support and friendship.

A children's book needs pictures and I will be forever grateful to local artist and good friend Sue Richards for agreeing to do the illustrations for the Mia books. I almost cried when I saw the first draft of the cover and some of the other water colour illustrations. Thank you, Sue!

Another big thank you goes to my editor Erin Britton. Thank you for all the advice and extra research you did to answer some of my questions. The final manuscript is a lot better, because of your input.

Turning a manuscript into a beautiful book is not an easy task and I am grateful to Robert Fowke and Ella Knight from YouCaxton Publications. I could not have done this without you.

Last but not least, I want to thank my family. I owe so much to my parents, who gave me the perfect childhood, allowing me to roam the forests, climb trees, ride ponies and find my own way in life. Thank you to my granddaughters Kayleigh and Jessica, who inspired me to write the stories. Thank you to Kathryn, who read them out loud during lockdown and the biggest thank you of all to my husband David, who supports all my crazy dreams. I hope that we get the chance to collect many more precious memories together.

About the author

J.K. Keane spent her early years running wild in the forests of her native Germany. When she was four years old, she decided that she was going to be an animal doctor. Her dream came true and she worked for more than twenty years as a vet, first in Germany and then in the UK. Now retired, she lives with her husband in Shropshire. When she's not busy writing, you'll probably find her exploring the local woods, looking for the best climbing trees or tracking the forest animals together with her grandchildren.

About the illustrator

Sue Richards has been drawing since a child and has kept a diary with sketches and a few words since she was a teenager. She always carries a sketch book when she travels to record her journeys. She has lived with her husband and children, working as a nurse in Shropshire, for many years.

During lockdown she started a journal to record the pandemic and told the journey that we all took into the unknown by sketching. Started in lockdown as a new avenue for her sketching, telling the story of Mia "has been so rewarding".

Printed in Great Britain
by Amazon

17204720R00077